A LITTLE BOOK OF
HOPE

MARIANA BORISOVA

Print information available on the last page

Rev. date: 06/27/2018

To order additional copies of this book, contact:
Xlibris
0800-056-3182
www.xlibrispublishing.co.uk
Orders@ Xlibrispublishing.co.uk

A LITTLE BOOK OF
HOPE

In memory of my grandmother, my white swallow of hope. You filled my soul with grace and love, and the amounts I now have are enough to give away.

Acknowledgements

If I hadn't seen the video about the blind boy explaining his way of life, I wouldn't have written this book of courage and hope.

First
He pampered me
With a hundred favours
Then
He melted me
With the fires of sorrows
After he sealed me
With the seal of love
I became him
Then
He threw my self out of me
I was nothing
You made me
Greater than a mountain …

—Rumi, "Alchemist"

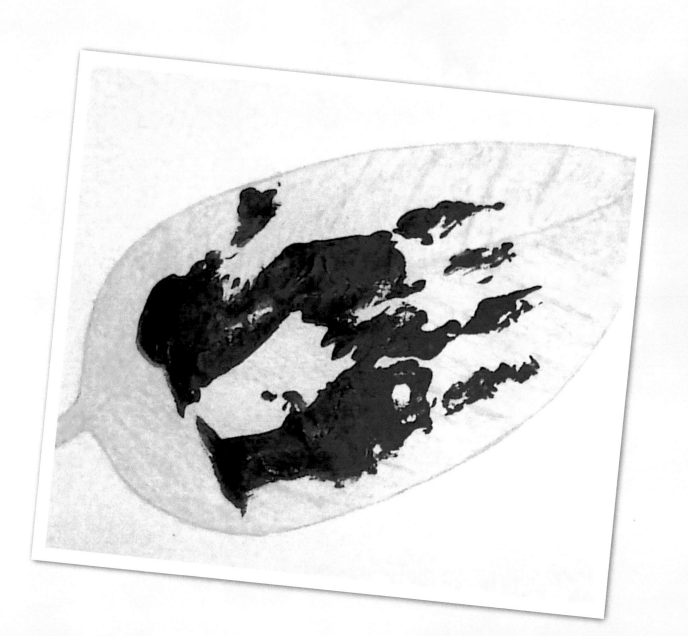

This story happened a long time ago, before suffering and wars. When the wars, destruction, and deluge passed, life went on in a smooth, calm manner towards the unforeseen future. One could tell that the happiness ruled, and the calm roamed in people's souls.

But time was of a stubborn nature. The calm and the silence were not its friends. In fact, it governed the people by its own laws. It was like a huge spider, abducting people with its web.

In the houses of some stolen souls appeared modern clocks that were tick-tocking rhythmically and unavoidably. People didn't move away their eyes from the hands of the clock. They rushed around and were always short of time.

The rest of them lived in an old-fashioned way. They made the time run around them. Yes, time was their servant. If you don't rush anywhere, why would you need a clock?

The children of those people happily played outside and stopped only if their circadian rhythm told them to do so. That would exactly coincide with the sun rolling away towards its rest.

Exactly then, groups of farmers carrying their spades covered in moist soil headed home through the village. At sunrise was their call, and they walked in groups towards the fields while singing, "The sun of the Lord can rise in our souls and rejuvenate them. I can, you can, he can, we can …" The air filled with energy in appreciation of the good words.

The sunrise and sunset had their own smells, and people were familiar with them. There wasn't that kind of nature recognition in the cities. There wasn't much time for that. Cities were as far from the villages as a desert could be from a sea.

In such a small, remote village lived Yano and his sister, Ina, who was two years younger. Yano was three years old when only he and his grandmother remained from his family. Everything happened in a short space of time, like living in a rollercoaster that stopped when someone had to come out or go in. Then with a screeching sound, it was on the move again and was not even finished when the ride had to stop again.

If destiny was establishing its rules, Yano was too young to know. One was certain that his grandparents were excited for their first grandson. The boy was healthy and quiet in his cot. He didn't even cry when feeding time was coming around. One and then two months passed in sheer happiness, and then the nurse came to check on him and the mother. All was good apart from one awkward thing. The child didn't look at and follow the toys she and the relatives used to attract his attention. His eyelids were half-closed, and this puzzled her. She gave them an appointment to see the doctor at the surgery.

It became clear that Yano was blind. When the worried parents asked how the blindness of their son could be cured, the doctor lifted his shoulders as if lost in answers. It seemed the easiest answer was simply to tell them to hope that a new treatment would be discovered.

The young parents saw all the famous doctors in the country, but the answer was negative and unclear, or they were advised to adapt and live with their son's disability. Yano's mother was hardly coping on her own, and so very often the grandmother would actively help in his upbringing. "Things somehow will work out for good," the old woman told her daughter, who breathed in her confidence in the future.

The young mother had calmed down and soon waited for her second child. Again it was happy commotion at home. This time it was going to be a girl, and they were going to name it Ina. The baby was born healthy and beautiful, but the mother became ill. Two months after giving birth, she passed away.

Yano's grandfather was badly affected by the loss of his daughter. His health went downhill. He complained from this and that, and his high blood pressure became hard to control. Within a year, he was gone.

Maria, Yano's grandmother, was completely lost from the family tragedy that occurred in a short amount of time. The sorrow ate at her. She became skinny, and the wrinkles on her face stood out as if asking for mercy. Only one little flame kept her existence, and it was Yano. She had to live because of him, to help him. Otherwise, he would be left on his own.

She felt that the father had different plans for his life in the future, and Yano was not included in them. He wanted to live in the town. "Everyone is going there," he used to tell her. He wanted to have his own home there and drive a car. Maria listened and didn't say anything. She wasn't hoping that something more would come out of him. This was his understanding of life.

Her first impression about him was that he was a cold man. She didn't see much of a heart there. When she'd met him the first time with her daughter, there had been some sort of pride in him that she hadn't liked. His parents were a bit wealthier than hers. This alone explained his ego. It was only at the wedding that Maria had met them.

Soon he found a job in the big city, and he prepared his and Ina's luggage. He said he was going to look after her and find her a good school, and Maria and Yano could come often to visit. That settled all. He added that this way, it would be easier for her to look after Yano, who needed more attention and time. His words were persuasive.

Ina didn't understand why her brother couldn't play with her. She didn't understand why he sat and moved his fingers across the white sheet of paper when there was nothing—no letters and no drawings. Ina had learned to write some letters, but her grandma didn't have time for her. She was always busy with Yano.

The old woman listened and thought that it was a good excuse for someone who wasn't a caring person, but she didn't say anything. She hoped that the change would be a new beginning for everyone. Thus, the children were to grow up separately. It was for their best, their father said. Maria wished she was strong enough to be around him.

Every time she looked at Yano's face, there was something that reminded her of her daughter. She didn't quite get what it was, but she knew it would come back to her. Maybe it was the way he moved his lips when he spoke or how he wrinkled his nose if he disliked something. He definitely had his dad's light chestnut hair. A thick fringe covered his eyebrows, shading his face. He was skinny, and his waistline had to be taken in every so often. Maria joked that she was afraid he would fly away with the lightest breeze. Perhaps for that reason, she always dressed him in bright colours. However, he knew if something happened to him, then his grandma would recognise him by the birthmark on his left cheek.

Yano grew up with the books that his grandmother read to him. They took him into their magic worlds that were so different from his. The countless adventures, the stories of bravery and compassion, and the happy endings came alive. Fables about people miraculously healed amazed him. The storybooks were so colourful, and his grandma wished that one day he would be blessed to see them. She also told him that one day he could also write a beautiful story.

But how, if the most interesting ones have already been written? thought Yano.

There was no way Yano could have known that an invisible pencil was writing his future story at a secret place in his heart. Day after day, it wrote down everything and hoped that one day, when Yano grew up, he would find it out and continue writing what the pencil had started.

Yano was almost seven years old and about to start school with his peers. He couldn't attend a special school for blind children because those were only in the towns. He went to town only with his dad, for eye check-ups. The recent one didn't bring any news. The doctor wanted to know if he could see anything behind his eyelids. Yano's answer was that something was moving, but he didn't know what it was. "Unclear outlines," the doctor translated to the father whilst writing it down in his notebook. His voice sounded unhelpful. After sending them off, he added, "Every blind person is a different case; however the best thing is to adapt to the situation. Then we will see how he is getting on in the future."

Because of the school, the doctor prescribed a special pair of darkened glasses. As soon as they were ready, they picked them up and then headed for the bus station.

On the street outside her house, Maria sat on the old wooden bench, waiting for them for more than an hour. She was a small woman—a fragile statue of a living martyr. Her shoulders bent slightly under the invisible weight of her almost seventy years. Her face wore the signs of worry and hard life, but her brown eyes spoke of a mellow soul. The dramatic expression of her face would have made her look even older, if she hadn't covered her grey hair.

Her neighbour, Grandfather Dobra, the oldest inhabitant of the village, was out sweeping the dust from his front door. When he saw Maria, he went to say hello and sat down next to her.

He was over ninety years old and had a slim and bony structure. Nevertheless, he was very energetic and possessed a rarely seen charitable character. His white hair, worn at shoulder length, framed a slightly darkened face and brown warm eyes from which pored a great amount of wisdom. He knew the healing properties of many herbs and plants one could find in the garden or in the wilderness. One could think of him as a walking library. People often sought him for advice on different illnesses and pains. He, the loner, helped as he could. He had lived in hard times and knew everything about the world.

"Maria, you have such a name, and the boy is blind," he used to say as if blaming her for the blindness of her grandson, especially shortly after Yano was born.

"What can I do, Grandfather Dobra? It is how he came to this world," she would say as if in excuse, not knowing why he would connect her name with the disability of her grandson.

"Could be healed but is too young," he would say.

Maria would shake her head and think, *The doctors can't heal my boy. How can Grandfather Dobra?*

This evening, while crying out her heart, Maria said," There is no healing for the boy, Grandfather Dobra. This is my torment."

"Maria, do not despair. You have to be strong." Then he murmured quietly to himself, "The boy is called upon …" In a minute, his voice returned, and he continued. "I'll tell you what you should do. Inspire in him big expectations and big hope for healing. Tell him not to worry about everyday life and he is going to be fine, I used to say to people years ago. Because the mind creates barriers, separates, and analyses. Hatred is rooted there, and all the bad in the world. That's why your boy has to do the opposite, to collect goodness. Suffering always gathers love and wins at the end. Those who suffer look for help beyond the borders of time and come back with the love, winning over, the time and worried. It depends on the man regarding what he is going to be."

Maria listened and struggled to get all the things Grandfather Dobra said that day, and the things he told her to do. She had heard and had read about those things from olden times, but believing in invisible things was the hardest part. She believed all those things that could be seen and touched. And because of Yano, she had to think of other things that she merely took as fairy tales. That day, Grandfather Dobra spoke about life, stars, and the world. He gave her books to read and educate herself.

Maria was ready to do anything for Yano. She used to care for her parents, both of them disabled. She got strong in hardship and misery. She was going to find some more strength to fight for Yano. As for the reading, she really didn't have the time. Since she was young, she had to work in the farming fields, and there wasn't time for anything else. She lived during the war and knew only how to care for the physical existence. She didn't know how to care for the soul.

It was mid-summer when Yano's future teacher came to meet him. She was young, and Maria saw uncertainty in her regarding the way she should go about Yano's blindness. Maria was happy for the technical staff she brought that would make the reading easier, but she also sensed that the techniques would break her communication with Yano. She hoped the boy would not to get too attached.

Grandfather Dobra's ideas roamed in her head, and she wanted to know whether she wouldn't be wrong to implement them and jeopardise her grandson's education. What if everything came out to be the way the old man explained to her regarding the possible healing of Yano?

Maria tossed and turned in bed during the night, her mind chewing on the possibilities. Her mind knit and unknit different outcomes.

Finally, she knew why Grandfather Dobra had connected her name with Yano's blindness. He had *that* Maria in mind—the one from the book, the mother of Jesus. It was clear that the woman who'd accepted the Holy Spirit would never have a blind child.

Maria wanted to know more about it, and her enthusiasm for reading increased. She wanted to catch up and find help now. She read until past midnight and couldn't fall asleep. During the day, tiredness overcame her, and the work in the garden was waiting to be done. Vegetables were their main dish, and she had to look after them. She preserved some for the winter; this was how they survived. Eggplants had to be shovelled, and tomatoes and cabbage had to be watered. On such busy days, she welcomed Yano's father and Ina's visits. Yano loved the chocolates from town, and Ina had brought to her brother the paper animals she'd made. She would leave them in his hands and describe them to him one by one.

This happy family picture lasted no more than a day and a half, and then Maria would catch up in the garden. She was thankful for that. After that, the silence would settle in the house, and there would be only the two of them to share it.

Yano wished he could see the face of the woman who was looking after him. She was like a mother to him, and although he didn't remember his, he knew his mum was daughter to his grandmother. *They must be somewhat similar,* he thought, and therefore he called her Mamie. He would touch her face, his fingers sinking in the wrinkles of her forehead, in the deep lines around her eyes and mouth. He heard people talking about the hardships she had passed, her strength and destiny. Much of it he didn't understand, but he was sure that his fingers had sensed the garden of goodness and love. It was enough for him.

One day while waiting on the queue at the grocery shop with Mamie, he heard how the people behind them were saying that his grandmother had a strong spirit. The tone of their voices and the word impressed him. He felt that this must be something nice and was happy for Mamie. It was more than politeness, and when they were back home, he asked her about it. She said that the spirit was something one couldn't see, but to make sure, she would have to ask grandfather Dobra. *So even people with normal eyesight can't see some things,* thought Yano.

Maria fell silent as the words of Grandfather Dobra emerged. "When you think of something nice and good, these thoughts have the power to help you. What are you thinking of is important. Your thoughts can do miracles. The Word is not in the mind—it is in the thoughts. Therefore teach the boy to think of the sky, of God. Teach him to use good words.

"Cut off the radio and television. The broadcasted words maybe no good, and they can clash with the good ones, make them appear darker, and take their strength away. Do you see what I mean? The good word can build up a double of Yano, with many lights and eyes up in the sky. Then this double would help Yano and give him new eyes. You have to teach him good, magnetic words, Maria," insisted the old man.

It wasn't going to be easy, and the worse was the lack of an action plan. She had terrible nights thinking and then falling asleep at dawn. The sun's first rays would wake her up.

Yano always knew when Mamie woke up early. The noise of slippers moving towards the fireplace in the kitchen was familiar. She would stop and stay there. The click of the lighter, then the sniffing. She liked to light a candle, she used to say to Yano.

It was clear Mamie was sad sometimes, and this ritual helped her. In the evenings she would put him in bed and go back to the fireplace, where she would read some books that had to be finished.

Yano didn't know what happened, but slowly Mamie heart hardened, and the sniffing stopped.

She would stay in the garden near the fence, and she spent time talking with Grandfather Dobra. The name *Dobra* meant goodness. *Maybe goodness attracts people together,* Yano thought.

"What I want to tell you, Maria, is that everything in this world is connected. But you don't read," he said with a bit of anger in his voice. "Everything that I told you some time ago could happen, but only if you are persistent. First, teach him to love the nature. He doesn't need anything else. It is well after his twelfth year when his prayers are going to be heard. Until then, you have to sow good seeds in his heart. Then the Word will make its way to his heart. Only the Word." He paused and then continued softly. "To be honest, the child is innocent. He is like that because to make us good people, and through his disability, the Lord works upon us, enlightens us. Do you know the story of Bartimaeus?"

"I don't. How can I, when there wasn't enough time for reading when I was young? I had read randomly from the big book. The stories were like fairy tales to me. I didn't think much about them," responded Maria.

"Mmm …" Grandfather Dobra pressed his lips together. "Then you have to read. I gave you some books. The world won't easily change for good. While there are walking blind, the blind are going to be born," he disclosed unhappily. Then he turned his back and walked away.

Maria stood there confused. She didn't know how to tell Yano all this. What were those magnetic words he'd told her a while ago? How could she find them? How could she stop Yano from reading his favourite stories and make him do things he may not want to do?

She decided some gardening may help. She had to create the circumstances and leave the rest in the hands of God.

That day, it was going to rain outside. Yano was at the table, reading something. Maria lit a candle, put it on the table in front of him, sat on the chair next to him, and told him to put his hands near the candle. Then she took his hands in hers and held them near the candle.

"Do you feel something?" Maria asked.

Yano felt a slight warmth coming from the candle. It wasn't like the warmth of the sun or the one coming from the fireplace.

"The fire is part of the nature. And nature can teach you a lot about the world. She is in it, and we are part of it."

Yano asked, "So, fire is within us?"

"Yes," Maria said. "Think about the words. Sometimes words can be like a fire. Bad words can destroy and burn. Good words can caress and embrace." "The flame is warm like you, Mamie, because you are good, and warmth is coming out of you," Yano interrupted. Then he asked, "Mamie, what's the colour of the candle flame? I want to know the colour of goodness."

Sometimes Yano's associations made her wonder from what world Yano had come. She sensed that it probably existed somewhere in the future. "The yellow and the red entwine in the flame. This is the colouring of the fire in the fireplace and the sun in the sky."

There was no way for Yano to understand colours; they couldn't be touched or felt. They were the hardest thing for Maria to explain. For this woman who knew lows in life and fought them, to not be able to have the slightest hope of coming out of the hole was a major hindrance. No one had been blind in her family before, so why Yano should be?

Silence settled in the room. Maria was helpless, but she couldn't give up now. Grandfather Dobra gave her hope, and she clung to it. It was good that he explained about the miracles in the big book, otherwise she would think that they were made-up stories, like most people. The hardest thing was to explain them to Yano and to make him believe in his healing. She was also worried she would get the translation wrong, and she therefore didn't have the strength to begin. She started cautiously. "Do you know that story about Robinson Crusoe?"

Yes, Mamie. I have read it many times, Yano thought.

Maria didn't wait for his answer and encouragingly said, "Alone on that island, he found a way to stay alive. He had a will to win. It would be good for you to acquire one."

"A will?" Yano repeated. "He was able to see, and he stayed alive."

"No, not because his eyesight, Yano. He found the way to survival." She was talking to herself now, lowering her voice. "When the bad happens, somehow you find the way." She remembered an old proverb that the good could grow out of the bad.

Maria's tension gave way to some positivity when she said, "My boy, you simply have to believe, and help will come for you. See, your granddad went in the big war. A bomb exploded close to him, and he survived. When he told us about it, he would always add at the end that angels had helped him. So miracles happen."

"They also existed within us," Grandfather Dobra echoed in her as a continuation of her husband's words. "Turn the coat inside out, Maria, and you will know." The voice of the old man cut through her thoughts. Maria thought a lot about it. She was certain that more than just a belief was needed, but it was something to begin with for now. 'Who have eyes to see and ears to hear," as was said in the book.

Yano thought that Mamie had changed a lot. She told him that he didn't need his audio books; he could have them later. He had to first believe in himself. It was going to be a long way, but at the end of it, a miracle could happen. And when it did, he would tell the whole world about it so that many like him could be healed.

Mamie's excitement about the future dragged Yano's heart towards it. Both of them happily imagined and enlivened another, different life. They continued to dream about it until they embraced, kissed on their cheeks, and wouldn't stop until their tears of delight merged.

After that, Mamie read stories about saints who had lived once but had suffered and were brave, and when they'd died, people had drawn halos around their heads. Their images entered many books and churches. Mamie said, "People should learn how to live their lives from them. They were lookalike angels, especially the most famous one. He told the people that it was not enough to be followed, but most important was to become like him, to feel what he felt."

Maria's concern was how to explain the rising of Jesus. Would Yano understand the most important aspect?

Everything that Grandfather Dobra explained to her—that in this life, people from their own suffering should work out their rising—was similar to the effort for the four walls of the pyramids to rise towards the top. What strengths were needed to gather the four ends of the cross in the middle? She remembered the bewilderment in grandfather Dobra's eyes.

Maria waved her thoughts away and decided she must tell Yano about the blind man called Bartimaeus, and how Jesus had healed him.

"Once, a long time ago, there was man who begged in the streets of the village where he lived. A saintly man, like an angel, used to go from village to village and help the most pure and needy. There were a lot at that time. When they heard he had come to their village, they began crying for help. Bartimaeus's cry for help was the strongest, his voice rising above the rest. People angrily told him to stop because they wanted to be heard too, but he continued. The saint man could not walk away. He went to the beggar and healed him."

"Why was only he helped?" Yano wanted to know.

"Because his cry for help was the strongest. You have to have a strong will and belief. And you must pray to this angel."

"Where did this angel come from?"

"It was sent by the one who people call God, who made everything in this world. The angels are helping because he sent them to his people."

"How can I ask him to help me?" asked Yano.

"Grandfather Dobra will advise us when the time comes. Now, it is time for something else." She took his hand, and they went out into the garden.

It was summer, and the garden was thriving. Aside from the vegetarian part, there was an area filled with flower plants. The aroma of chrysanthemums stood out. They were taller than Yano. Maria told him he could stretch his arms out and embrace them. They would be happy if he did that. Yano did embrace their stems, and as he let them go, their round, leafy heads touched his face. Yano smiled.

"In the pot here, we have Ficus benjamina," Maria said. "It has grown as strong as a tree and always has green leaves. It doesn't need much care—a little shade when it is hot, and watering." Yano touched the leaves and sensed their smoothness. It was clear they were wider than his palm. Every day he measured his hand with it.

"They like the gentle touching, talking, and watering," Maria taught him. Yano had his own watering pot, and with Mamie's help, every day he checked on them, asked them how they were, and watered them. He learned confidently to walk amongst them. After all, they stayed at one and the same place, and there was no danger for him to walk over them or hit himself, as he did sometimes in places unknown. He spoke to them as friends would do.

Days were long in the summer. After dinner, Yano wanted to draw on paper his new friends. Mamie liked his drawings, however he had to improve by doing it every day.

She made him touch the bowl full with fruits on the table and draw it. It was difficult. Day after day, Yano improved and was able to fit his drawing within

the paper sheet. Mamie's mood grew day by day. Even Yano could hear her humming a melody, and he would feel elated. It made him double his drawing efforts.

Sometimes he wondered where Mamie's strength came from. Yano thought it was from the old chest of drawers that she would often open. There were stored heavy coats from the war, Mamie explained. Yano liked to stroke the smooth metal buttons. Mamie said they were made of iron and were strongly attached to the fabric. *As if they always had to be there to remind of their strength,* Yano thought. It seemed that Mamie also had some kind of metal in her body that gave her strength and kept her from falling down.

Maria entered the house and made sure Yano was all right. Then she went into the bedroom and opened the old chest of draws. While standing there, strange thoughts overcame her. Maybe Grandfather Dobra was right, saying that her ancestors were warriors. It was sin to kill others. Maybe because of that, Yano was like that this … "Until the people realise that and leave the wrongdoings, change won't come," she heard the wise man's voice say.

Maria decided to throw away the old coats, to stomp on the patriotism, so that she could make room for the God in her house. What was done was done; it stayed in the past. Now, she wanted to live with the hope.

She grabbed them all, made a fire in the garden, and burned them. Her eyes followed the black smoke rising towards the sky, and she hoped she had done good.

Yano sensed that Mamie became softer after that, as if the metal came out of her body and trusted its existence to another force. Another, different strength poured out of her.

In the summer, neighbours often came into their house. Some of them would bring apples and grapes from their harvest, and Maria would give them produce from her garden: tomatoes, cucumbers, and eggplants. After that, the conversation would go on about preserves and recipes. At the end, when the visitors were about to go home, they would ask how Yano was.

Maria didn't complain and self-pity anymore. She joyfully aid that Yano was going to regain his sight one day. "Bravo. It is nice to see that there is hope," they would say. They suggested she tell him real-life stories. But Maria was certain that if Yano was healed, he would see the bad in life.

Yano listened and wondered from where did Mamie found this confidence to talk to people like that. She even told them about the flowers and the progress of his drawing.

Yano was happy for this positive mood at home, and he was happy when

Mamie got him involved in gardening even more. She made him help her saddle small pepper plants, telling him to bore his finger in the soil. In that hole, she put the roots of the tiny pepper plant. Yano was overwhelmed at all things he could do in the garden.

But drawing was his passion, and his efforts paid off. Soon he had managed to fit two objects on the paper, starting with the one that was farther away. Then he measured the distance of the nearest object with fingers and transferred the distance onto the paper, punching the paper with the tip his finger to mark where he was going to start. He always gave his father and Ina a drawing to take home.

Most of all, Yano wondered how to draw himself in full height. First he drew a vertical line on the paper, and then a horizontal one that crossed the first one. Not sure he positioned it right, he would do another one over it, and another one. There was not enough space to draw the legs, and his pencil would continue out of the paper edge.

"Mamie, I drew myself!" he cried proudly.

Yano couldn't see the tears that came down Maria's face. She saw the several horizontal lines that crossed over the vertical one, as if in attempt to delete it. The vertical line of a cross, a human being that was not allowed to be.

In Yano's drawing, it looked he had denied himself. The association alarmed her. She wanted her grandson to have a fulfilled life, to have an independent life like everyone else. He was not a mistake. She would help him to see the world, to transform and rise from his cross. She believed in that. In the evenings, she continued with her readings, and the Word melted her heart. "I tell you the truth, he who says to the mountain, be taken up and cast into the sea, and does not doubt in his heart, but believes that what he says is going to happen, it will be granted him." The words of Mark made her believe in their enormous power. Her heart knelt in front of God.

One day Maria saw Grandfather Dobra working in his garden. She went near the fence and said, "Grandfather Dobra, tell me something, please. How can I find a powerful word? The prayers as they are in the book are too long and hard for a boy at this age to understand."

The old man came closer to the fence and said, "Maria, the Word was with God, and he created the existence of all beings in all forms, as we can see. They are coded information of God's love, and light is present in their making. The word *light* must be a powerful one. Light is everything. Find more words like it and repeat them because repetition is happening. Strong words work together and attract forces. They can get your grandson out of the darkness." Grandfather Dobra's eyes sparkled from excitement.

Maria made the sign of a cross and said, "Thank you. God bless you for your goodness and help."

Early September summoned children to school. Yano was excited too. In class, he couldn't do much except for listening to the teacher, and at home he did some reading. Maria was worried more about his positive mood than his lessons, the books in Braille, and other tools. She piled them at one side of the table as if they were never to be touched. Instead of these books, she taught Yano the good words. It was true that Yano was going to fall behind his classmates, but if he regained his sight, wouldn't that be the greatest thing in the world? A wave of excitement went through Maria's body. After that, he would have plenty of time to catch up with school material.

"Mamie, why can I not listen to some stories?" he would ask while his fingers reached towards the audio files.

"You shouldn't mix the good words with those from your stories. You have to follow your first wish, and it is to give a chance for the healing process to start. Later, there will be plenty of time for everything else," Maria was adamant. How could she explain to her grandson that she wanted him to be in the wave of the excitement that Jesus brought to the world, rather than in the world of pleasure and short-lived happiness?

Yano's first days of school were hard. Being different made him sad. He said to Maria that he wanted to run and play outside in the school ground with the rest of the children. Instead, he sat on his own in the classroom. Maria told him to not worry about anything; otherwise, the sorrow wouldn't allow the healing to happen. "Repeat in your mind the good words. They will deal with the sorrow," she reminded.

Maria often allowed Yano to visit his friend Toni at Toni's house. Years ago, the mothers of the two boys were friends. At school, the boys sat next to each other. Toni understood Yano's needs and how he could help. For Maria, this was a relief.

Toni played piano. When Yano came, he allowed him to press the keys. They imagined they were performing. A cacophony of sounds threatened to bring down the house until the door opened, and Toni's mum appeared. The concert wouldn't be over. The boys excused themselves and went out into the garden, where their happy laughs continued. Toni always walked Yano home, some fifty meters away.

Halfway there stood a tall tree. On its top was a big nest, and each spring a family of storks found accommodation and raised their young ones there. Toni would always stop and exclaim when he saw a stork in its nest. They stayed there, and Toni explained what he saw and how the stork fed the chicks with its beak, possibly carrying small fish from the nearby river. Adults stopped and enjoyed watching them too. They knew that when summer was over, the birds would fly away.

"Mamie, the stork is here again!" exclaimed Yano upon entering the house. Maria was cleaning the fireplace. Spring had come; the fireplace would be clean for the next winter.

She froze for a moment. There was a legend that the storks brought babies to families who desired to have one. The bird would drop them through the chimney. It was like Father Christmas and his way of throwing presents to children through the chimneys. Maria also remembered the tiny book explaining that the invisible energy surrounding us could make anything happen.

Yano broke into her thoughts. "Mamie, don't you think that the stork who brought me to Mum and Dad came a bit earlier?"

"Why, son?" she said, looking at him.

Yano found the small wooden chair near the door, sat, and continued. "Because when I was taken from the nest in the sky, my eyes weren't ready yet."

"Could be," returned Maria thoughtfully. She added, "It could be that the bird has done it on purpose."

"Why so?"

"To give you a lesson. Maybe you should learn the way to the nest in the sky, go there and get them by yourself." Her voice was grave.

"How can I find the way if I can't see? How can I see the bird and follow it?"

"Don't pity yourself, but believe that you can, and you will find the way. You have to try different things. Help will come spontaneously from within. With all the shows that move behind your eyelid, tell them in your mind to gather in the form of a small dot. Put your finger on the top of the pencil."

She gave him one, and Yano touched it. "See? You can do this exercise. The tip is as small as a dot. Millions of them, called atoms, make up our bodies." Maria recalled Grandfather Dobra's books. "They can group together and make our own double above, in the sky—something that we can call our star, or our angel. He is the one who likes to hear the good words every day. Surely the help is going to come to you."

"Yes, like the story of the blind man you have told me about."

"Yes, Yano."

In the evenings when they went to bed, Maria told him to think about the light and to ask the light to come until he fell asleep. She would start whispering, "Light, light, love, love," and Yano repeated after her and waited for a light the size of a dot to appear behind his lids and take him to his angel.

In the daytime, Yano found himself thinking about the light and wondering how it looked? He knew that the sun's rays warmed his body, gently touching his skin. Yano felt that out in the sun, his mind easily started to think about it, and he started whispering, "Light, light, love, love. Love is coming." Yano believed it was going to come.

A harmony of thoughts and feelings was building in his body—a kingdom in which he lived in constant bliss and joyful expectation.

Day and night merged. Yano's heart became a ball of light, and love and rapidly increased. "Words are powerful. They can make or destroy. Get the strongest one to help you. The little dot of light will show you the world," echoed Maria's words in his head.

"What about colours, Mamie?" asked Yano.

"Everything …"

Since then, Yano had lost interest in the storybooks on the bookshelf. Only the words that can make the big explosion, the big change from within, could bring the light to him, Mamie told him. "What is an explosion?" he asked.

"It is something like the crackling sound of the wood, burning in the fireplace. It is being changed by the fire into something else," Maria explained.

But the fire in the fireplace gives a lot of warmth, and you can burn, Yano thought. He didn't have the courage to ask if he was going to survive in a big explosion, where there was a fire. He embraced Mamie instead. She gave him strength that kept away every thought of fear and doubt.

Yano would go into the garden, and while near the garden fence, he asked

Grandfather Dobra to come. The old man became his dearest friend. Upon hearing the coming steps, Yano squeezed his hand through the hole of the metal net and searched for Dobra's hand. Touching was Yano's language. The old, bony hand was similar to his grandmother's. Yano knew they both spoke the same language, the language of goodness.

He thought about Grandfather Dobra as of one of the saints from the books, and he liked what the man told him. Grandfather Dobra told him that when he was his age. mornings after waking up. he used to say the following, "Thank you, Lord, for everything you have given me and have taught me. Thank you, Lord, for the good will you have towards us. We know that you are all-merciful, all-truthful, and all-wisdom." The voice of Grandfather Dobra was full of inspiration and pathos. Yano absorbed every word and applied everything that was good for him.

Maria notified the old man of the change in Yano. His heart was overflowing with joy about the boy. Since then, they met often in the garden, and Grandfather Dobra gave him special word formulas, which Yano had to remember and repeat every day. Yano didn't understand what exactly the Lord was, but the Word was from the good ones, and it could only help him. Also, all helpers of the people, the angels, were with him. His mother, whom he didn't remember, also went up there to them.

Yano trusted Grandfather Dobra, and soon the communication of these two souls turned into a game.

For example, instead of "hello" or "good morning", Yano would say to the old man, "Lord, teach me to see with your eyes."

Grandfather Dobra nodded with appreciation. Instead of "Hello. Yano", he said, "Lord, give me the exact remedy. Give me yourself." Then he explained, "The Lord has made the world, and everything is in him, all remedies. He can give you everything, if you know how to ask."

Yano remembered it. After that, he thought of a new one and went to tell to

Grandfather Dobra. He didn't miss the opportunity to exchange formulas when the man was out in his garden. While standing near the fence, he would say, "Lord, I am giving myself to your love. Let it heal me and guide me."

The quick response was, "Lord, live within me!"

The game went on for the whole summer. School closed for the summer holidays. Yano would often accompany his grandmother to the grocery store. One day, Mamie told him that Grandfather Dobra was waving at them from the opposite sidewalk. For Yano, this meant the game was on. This time, Grandfather Dobra was quick. "Lord, you heal this soul in the best possible way!"

Yano remembered it straight away. He thought the man would like his formula. Then he stopped and shouted towards him, "Lord. bless me to see you, for I will be transformed!"

Many of the pedestrians around them stopped, made the sign of the cross, and exclaimed, "Bravo, bravo!" Some of the villagers knew what would happen when the boy and the old man were around, and they waited patiently to hear the new prayers. The intensity and power struck them, enlivened them. Older women would tell Maria, "We wish him all the best."

The list of formulas became longer day by day, and Yano told them to himself from first to last one and added a new one. Days flew away like a flock of birds. Yano didn't even notice his ninth birthday and the beginning of the new school year.

He had to wake up earlier to say all his formulas before going to school. He loved them so much that there was no way he would go out without spending the right amount of time for his new ritual. They were his friends. He felt them close to his heart, as an invisible connection with the Lord.

The weather was changing, and again this year, the storks flew away to the south, leaving the village to stand there alone as an orphan. Days became shorter and darker. Flocks of ravens roamed the sky, looking for food in the nearby fields. The forecast was for heavy snow, unseen till now. Yano's father and sister didn't want to risk the roads and were not coming.

One December morning, the village woke up covered with snow higher than a human. Maria told Yano that she had never seen so much snow in all her life. Villagers cleared the main road to the grocery shop, the school, and the church. Maria came back home frozen and told Yano that the roads turned into paths, and on both sides the piled snow had become a two-metre-high fence, touching the houses behind it. The icy fence breathed cold and stiffened the bones of the pedestrians. Temperatures remained below zero and were expected to fall.

It was announced that the school was going to close because of the harsh weather.

This day, Maria took Yano to school and said to the teacher that she wasn't going to meet him after school. She had made an arrangements for him to go home with Toni. Yano knew that Mamie was going to be busy at home cooking. She was going to attend a funeral ceremony in the church, and food had to be taken there.

Mamie said to him in the morning that she wasn't sure he had to go to school at all, but she had spoken with Toni's mother the previous day. "The bad weather shouldn't be an excuse for us," she said.

Around the end of the second lesson, Toni felt unwell, and his head relaxed on the table. The teacher felt his forehead and said it was too hot. She told him he can go home. Toni put on his jacket, took his rucksack, and left. It was the toll of the bell that reminded the teacher about Yano. She had to take him home.

After the last lesson, she told him to wait for her in the room. Yano waited and waited. Minutes seemed like hours. He thought that he didn't want to be a problem for the teacher. Maybe she wanted to go back home as soon as possible in this bad weather. Yano thought if he made it to his home on his own, Mamie would be proud of him. There weren't cars on the road—nothing to be scared of. He was going to count the steps. He used to do that many times.

He opened the heavy classroom door and listened. It was quiet. He set off towards the entrance, walking close to the corridor wall. He walked by a couple of doors and heard a notice coming from one of the rooms. Maybe pupils from upper class had more lessons. The silence of the school yard encouraged him, and he walked confidently towards the metal front gate of the school. He touched the icy metal, and left the school. The snow crunched under his boots. One hundred and twenty steps, before the turn to the left. Then it was going to be the same amount to his front door. He took his left hand out of his pocket and touched the snow fence.

"Oh, Yano, are you on your own?" a woman asked him while walking in the opposite direction.

"I am going home. I will be all right," he said with confidence. Then he continued, turning to the left. It was not that far now. Runners would make it in seconds. His worry was not the time. He had to watch out for the ending.

The noise of heavy steps stumping in the snow came from behind him. Their sudden appearance surprised him. He could usually recognise the noise from afar. Mamie used to read to him about avalanches, which could fall on people in the mountains. He wondered whether the snow surrounding him could start falling on top of him. He shuddered at the thought and slowed down. The heavy steps came close but didn't go away. Yano wished they were gone.

Something hit him on his back, and he fell on the ground, burying his face in the snow. The knocks continued.

"I hate you, I hate you!" shouted the attacker. Yano recognised the voice of the big boy from upper classes who bullied the younger pupils. The boy held him down in the snow. Yano couldn't shout; his mouth was filled with snow. The strong hand held the collar of his jacket, pulling him backwards.

Yano was on his knees, trying to stand up. His boots slipped every time, and he had no grip. The boy kept pushing him to the ground at every attempt.

All of a sudden, the torment stopped. Yano moved his hands around to find his glasses. He wanted to continue his path without going the direction wrong.

But his attacker wasn't finished yet. The hand held the collar of the jacket and his top from the back. Yano's skin was bare, and he felt touch of the cold air. But this was not the end. The big boy started to fill his back with snow. Yano realised that while he'd struggled to stand up, the boy had prepared the balls. Now the hard balls were rolling down his back, sticking their icy surface on to his warm skin, making his breath and heart stop. Yano felt that he had a body which was empty from the inside. The snow reached his neck, and this was when the attacker had enough and left him alone.

Icy hoops twisted Yano's head while he walked slowly towards home. He wanted to cry, but the pain from the event stiffened him. He couldn't understand why he deserved that. Somehow he didn't want to know. The cold blocked his thoughts. He left them for later. Finally he opened the front door of his house. It took him ages to move one foot after the other.

He entered the kitchen. The warm air coming from the fireplace hit him. He realised he had no strength for anything, and he stayed there near the door. He wanted to say something but had no voice. He heard running water and pots being washed; Mamie was at the sink. She had her back towards him and didn't hear when he came in. He felt his cheeks burning, and his eyes too, threatening to come out of their place. His back was aching as never before. Under his jacket, water drizzled down and made a paddle on the floor.

"Yano!" Mamie's voice came to him as if from afar. "Who did this to you?"

"Mamie …" Yano almost whispered, and he relaxed in Mamie's hands. He felt the warm clothes on his body, but they couldn't warm him up. She put him into bed and said she was going to make him a cup of tea.

After that, he didn't know anything. The house became tiny. He was so tall now, and he could reach and touch the top of the trees. Sometimes he could hear Mamie's voice and the voices of others, but he sunk again and went somewhere far away, and he didn't hear them anymore. He felt as a part of the air, wind, and the sky, part of everything around him. He was connected to the universe. He realised he'd had the knowledge about all this, but now he sensed it and experienced it.

Suddenly some voices he recognised called upon him, and he felt he was being turned around in bed. He wondered whether it was day or night. He was thirsty, but he couldn't say so, and he sunk again and again in the fairy world, where he sensed connectivity, closeness, and love. He sensed that he was big and flew through the air like a balloon. There was so much space, and he wasn't knocking himself on sharp corners. He didn't fall down as he used to in Mamie's house. He was floating without the need of touching.

He sensed the buzzing of a bee around him and was happy he was not alone. The buzzing became an audible whisper. "I am the angel of the white light—Uriel. Try to see me with the secret eye, which is situated between your eyebrows. Think of me as a dot, as little as the tip of a pencil, and repeat the word *light*."

Yano did as he was told, his attention on the place between his eyebrows. He repeated the word. In a while, a little trembling light appeared there, in the place between his eyebrows. Yano told her to increase, and she became bigger and continued to grow. It became bigger than an apple and grew until it enveloped him in its white light. Light surrounded him. The light came to him, and Yano was happy. He was hovering in this sea of light and realised that he could see around. Dots of lights came together and spread, outlining the form of a man. Yano thought that this must be Uriel, and he thanked him in his mind. He answered him that they looked alike. Yano liked that and paid attention to what Uriel said.

"White colour consists of the colours of the rainbow. I can show them to you."

At that moment, the dots started to move in different directions, and the human form disappeared in the air. Looking out for him, Yano felt he moved downwards, and thoughts about airplanes came into his mind. All of a sudden, his movement stopped, and he scanned around. He was surrounded by objects coloured in different colour. He heard the same buzzing sound, and in front of him appeared the outline of the angel of blue colour as he presented himself. He came closer and touched his forehead with his hand, and Yano instantly knew what Rafael was about to tell him: that in the blue around him, he could also trace tiny streaks of gold. Therefore when Yano drank from the blue light, he was going to have gold in his body, and his body would never tarnish. Yano remembered that. He didn't understand how he could drink if he didn't feel like a human being, but rather like a huge, balloon-like creature. He didn't know whether he had a mouth at all. For sure, he had numerous eyes all over his body because he could see in all directions in no time. The high blue mountains, blue rivers, and blue trees with long, golden-bluish branches draw his attention. He stood there in amusement. The voice of Rafael came to him and told him to breathe the right way when he wanted to see him and help him.

Yano breathed deeply as he was told, but instead of the breathing lesson, he found himself falling downwards, and with this movement his size decreased. He disliked the sudden change, but he found himself in a new surroundings. This time the colour was again different. He saw beautiful flowers, mountains, and trees painted in this colour. He wondered what it might be.

Yano sensed that his palms were warming up, and it reminded him about the warmth coming from the flame of the candle and the warmth coming from the fireplace. Warmth spread throughout his body. He guessed the colour, but the buzzing of the bees surrounded him. "Look with your secret eye. Otherwise, there is no other way to know what colour you see."

Yano concentrated his attention to the place between eyebrows, thinking of the little light dot and asking to appear. As previously, dots appeared in millions, regrouped, and reshaped. They outlined the shape of a man, and he spoke to Yano. "I am Michael, the angel of the red light. I have the best shield. Think of me when you seek help and protection. Call me if you need me." Yano sensed a wave of warmth coming out from him. He could have thought of it as a fatherly embrace, but Yano didn't have a memory of such. This warmth reminded him of Mamie's embrace instead.

Yano understood that everything in the world was connected. His thought broke off as he tried to get what Michael was telling him. "You are different now."

What did it mean? Yano thought as he sensed that the descent continued without a warning. He felt the rough force that sucked him downwards, decreasing in size.

Suddenly he stopped, and all around him was in a different colour than the previous one. This time Yano didn't wait for a reminder, and he looked towards the secret eye, repeating the thought, "What is this colour?" Soon a light dot appeared, increased in size, and formed an unclear form in a huge ball. From there a human image appeared in front of him. His eyes looked at him warmly. Yano heard, "I am Gabriel, and my colour is green. Are you thirsty? Drink from my water, and you aren't going to be thirsty, aren't going to be thirsty …" It echoed in his heart. He thought that the flowers may need watering—his flowers. Yano saw himself in a green colour. Now that he was smaller, he could do that. He knew the colour of the leaves, of the forest, of the mountains, and he felt one with them more than ever. Mamie also used to explain to him about the colours. Everything fell into place.

His favourites were blue and green. He immediately saw himself in overflowing aqua blue and green. Yano realised something changed in him. He felt he was much better than before, but he didn't know in what sense.

In a few seconds, everything darkened and disappeared.

He opened his eyes. He was on his own and was in his bed. Where did all colours go? He lifted his arm and looked at it. Was this him? Yano knew that he could see. There was not much time to look around the room, because the door opened. Yano put his arm back under the cover. Half closing his eyes, he watched a woman come to him. He didn't move.

"Yano," the woman whispered. Her hand touched his forehead. Yano knew the skin of Mamie's palm.

"Mamie," he said with a weak voice. He opened his eyes, looked at the woman, took out his hand, and reached for hers. "Mamie, I see you. I see you now."

In her joy, Maria staggered. The miracle had happened in her house! She rushed to help her grandson from the bed. He had lost weight and was very weak. For more than a week, he hadn't put anything in his mouth. He raved day and night and was thirsty, but he didn't drink from the water bottle Maria had given him. In her despair, Maria thought that her boy was so disappointed from life on earth, from people's bad manners, that he wouldn't come home again.

Yano had an allergy to the antibiotics prescribed, which could have healed his frozen body much sooner. Maria warmed his feet when they seemed to be too cold. When his forehead was burning from the temperature, she dressed him with clothes wet with vinegar to lower the heat. She prayed for him to come back to her. Now he was here, healthy as ever. A newborn to this world.

Yano felt different, grown-up. They embraced each other. He wanted to see his flowers and water them. Usually during the winter they only kept the lemon tree and the ficus plant, indoors. Yano went to them and spoke to them. "You helped me. Thank you." For Yano, everything on earth was a living thing and needed attention. He had gathered the love from infinity, and it lived in him.

Maria watched him with apprehension and asked herself how the world would accept him now.

Yano didn't know that all angels from above watched him and wished him good luck. He didn't learn all the colours of the rainbow, but at least he had something to begin with.

"Mamie, ask Grandfather Dobra to come."

The three of them sat around the fireplace in the evening on the following day. The days after were not enough to talk about the beautiful world on the earth and in the sky. Yano, believing and carrying the hope in his heart, finally had gathered the sky and earth in himself. He lived a new life with a joy in his heart, which he wanted to share with everyone. However, he didn't expect to be understood. It was clear the hardest thing in life was to be like the earth and like the sky—to be a conscious heart.

Angels saw his concerns, and because of children like him, they wanted the planet to become a planet of conscious hearts. They prayed from above, and Yano, Grandfather Dobra, and Maria did the same. This prayer was one of the rare moments of harmony between earth and sky.

Angels wished the heart and soul of this child to remain unchanged, to stay in the eternity, to be one with the universe. People tended to change and limit time to their vision of the world. Life was parsed into hours and minutes, and people died within this time partition. The infinity was slowly diminishing, and the world of miracles and hope became foreign and forgotten to the earth's inhabitants.

What about Yano? They marked him in order to find him easily, and they hoped the boy wouldn't forget about them. Now it was time for him to start writing his own story.

Then they headed above and promised themselves to look down from time to time at Yano, because he was part of them now.

Printed in the United States
By Bookmasters